For Peter and Blue

All right reserved. Published by Scholastic Inc.,
Publishers since 1920, by arrangement with Bloomsbury Publishing Plc.
SCHOLASTIC and associated logos are trademarks and/or registered trademarks of Scholastic Inc.

Library of Congress Cataloging-in-Publication Data available

ISBN 0-439-20670-7

10 9 8 7 6 5 4 3 2 1   00 01 02 03 04

Printed in Singapore
First American printing, October 2000

My Duck

by Tanya Linch

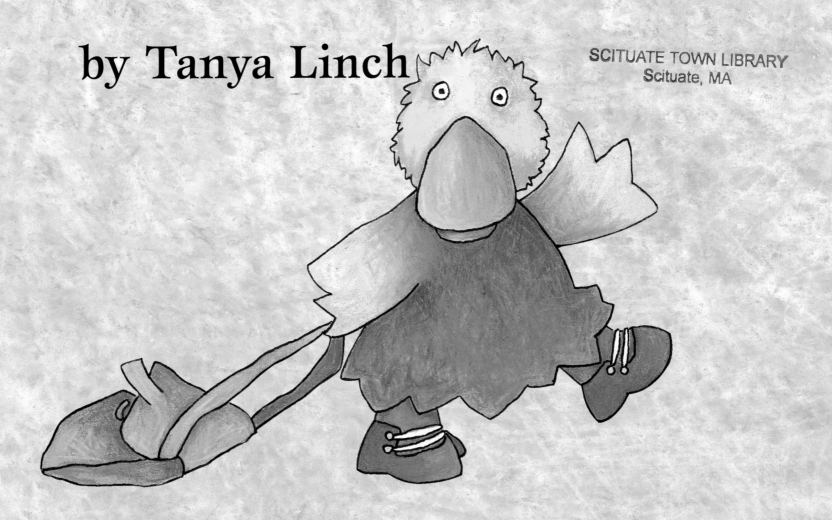

So I had to explain to my duck that I was starting my story again.

"But I've already packed my sandwiches," he said, and off he went.

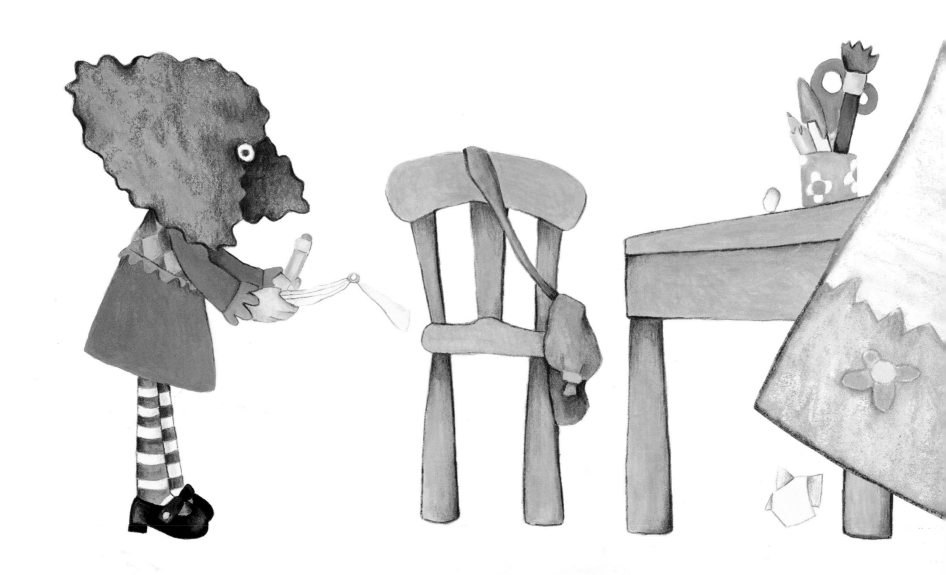

My second story was about how I get to school, so I drew the tree in the middle of the road that we pass every morning in the car.

"Trees don't grow in the middle of the road!" said my teacher. "Go and start again!"

By the time I got back to my desk to start again, something very strange was happening.

My duck was sitting under our tree and waving at me!

I told my duck that he couldn't possibly stay there because I was starting my story again.

"But there is nowhere else to eat my lunch!" he told me, and carried on anyway.

My third story was going to be about a little girl who could fly, and I told my teacher about her.

"Little girls don't fly!" said my teacher. "Try another story!"

But I hadn't finished drawing my little girl, and she only had one wing.

When my duck saw the little girl, he said, "She's nice. Can she be my friend?"

I explained to my duck that it was impossible because I was starting my story again.

"But I've got no one else to play with," said my duck, and he asked the little girl if she wanted to share his lunch.

Before I could do anything about it, the little girl hopped
and skipped and flew over to where my duck was sitting.

Meanwhile, I started my fourth story, which was about my trip to the zoo, and I drew all of the animals I had seen.

This is a story my teacher will like, I thought,
and I was just about to show it to her when I noticed my duck
and the little girl eating their lunch next to the lion's cage.

On the way, they passed the food stand that I had drawn, and they helped themselves to milk shakes and cupcakes, and then they sat on the wall to watch the people go by.

I tried again to explain that this story would only work if they would leave, and I promised that I would start another story, just for them.

"But this is my home now," said my duck.
"I'm not leaving again."
   The little girl nodded
her head in agreement.

But if you ever go to the zoo and see a duck with shoes on and a little girl with one wing, please . . .

don't tell my teacher!